# THE HUI

## *by*
# The Snark

### An Apology,
### in Eight Fits and a Start
### and an End

⚜

### Foreword
### *by*
### JJS

### Portraits & Panorama
### *by*
### Xanna Eve Chown

First published in 2020 by Doplin Books, Brighton.

Production Editor: Xanna Eve Chown
Copyright: JJ Secker © 2020

ISBN 9798601805179

*To my twin brother*
*DEOGRATIAS RILCHIAM SNARK*
*Sorely Missed*
*(But he did and I did not)*

(TWS 189_)

ₐᵢₑ ✤ ₐᵢₑ

*To his twin brother*
*THEOPHILUS WILLARD SNARK*
*Substantially Untried*
*(But now in a Higher Court)*

(IJS 2018)

# Dead Definition

If you have read this opus you will know whodunnit and how he dunnit. But **why**? I showed the text to a Professor of Psychiatry and asked if there was a term for such actions in the field of Ludothanatology. He said that The was unique, but deserved a term of his own which he coined from his 'nom de folie' in the Hunting.

So perhaps you would like to work out what this was. Take one letter from each crew member's name and rearrange them to make a ten letter word. The answer is unique, apart from the obvious interchangeability of identical letters.

## WHAT WAS THE SNARK?

HINT: The letters are arranged in the order of the crew on the Malcontents page. The solution is given at the end of this book.

JJS

# Malcontents

The chapters on this page are deliberately out of sequence.
IF YOU HAVE NOT READ THIS POEM AND
YOU WANT TO IDENTIFY THE SNARK BY
MEANS OF SHERLOCK (OR SHEER LUCK)
– DO NOT EXAMINE THIS PAGE!

# Foreword

*A few years ago I inherited, inter alia, the horsehair chest that originally belonged to my Great Great Great Uncle Theophilus. He was a greatly respected elderly gentleman who died in 1899 in his old home of Twasme Lodge, now a highrise block of flats. He had had a twin brother Deogratias (they called each other The and Dee) who was the victim of an atrocity that was never solved (until perhaps now, according to a gratuitous verse in this book). He married, somewhat late in life, an American called Eliza Borden. Little is known of this lady save for the fact that she had a niece named after her who later received a certain amount of notoriety in the U.S.*

*The was a widely travelled person in the 19th Century. His chest contained:*

*1. Logs of his voyages, which were privately published by the family between the Wars as Extraordinary Exploits of an Exceptional Explorer.*

*2. Items of clothing from around the world, the best of which had been donated to an anthropological museum in Cambridge.*

*3. Heath Robinson contraptions which I had believed naively were early autoerotic impedimenta. It would seem, having scanned the narrative in this volume, that I was even more naive than I thought.*

*Earlier this year I was reading an article on taxidermy and it occurred to me that the 'horsehair' came from a different animal altogether. I have never determined which, but while I was cutting a strip of it from the inside of the chest for analysis there was a muffled click and a concealed compartment slid open. It contained the following amazing – albeit gruesome – manuscript purporting to describe the true tale of 'The Hunting of the Snark'!*

*This saga written by Lewis Carroll and published in 1876, a Hundred Plus years ago, has long fascinated me; not just because of the family connections with the name but the sheer majesty of the adventure, comparable to a Viking Edda.*

*I had always assumed that it was pure fantasy, but this manuscript throws a startling new light on the story.*

*It would seem from the author's preface that he not only knew Lewis Carroll but had a love/hate relationship with him that lasted a lifetime. In the unlikely event that you have purchased this volume without having read its precursor I suggest that you correct this omission.*

*It is available on a number of sites on the internet, and has been issued in many forms. Apart from the magnificent original plates by Henry Holiday the definitive version is illustrated by John Vernon Lord (2006), the splendidly offbeat by the quirky Byron Sewell (1974) and my personal favourite by the talented John Minnion (1976).*

*I present the manuscript as it was found except for the correction of a small number of spelling errors; one cannot correct the grammar of poetry. The photograph mentioned at the start of the poem has not been passed down, unfortunately; but I have commissioned a series of interpretive pictures to augment the text from a talented established illustrator who is, herself, a Great Great Great Great Niece of Theophilus.*

*The opus is described as an Apology by the author. This is the old form of Apologia: a justification of one's motives or acts. Having said that, there is no hint of regret, or indeed explanation, for the multiple murders or casual anthropophagy in a text that is shocking even in these desensitised days. Perhaps this lack of sentiment is itself the justification. In 'The Hunting of the Snark' ten ordinary men, a true cross-section of Society, expend a large amount of effort in hunting creatures that they had never seen and who "do no manner of harm" according to Carroll. They intend to capture them or slaughter and eat them ("a flavour of Will-o'-the-wisp") with emotionless efficiency.*

*In the same way, maybe, a subspecies of Homo call-him Predatrix may be prepared to deal with Homo so-called Sapiens. Perhaps we should contemplate the old phrase 'Let us Prey'. But this is my own rationalization and probably without relevence.*

There is no indication that this account is fraudulent. From a reference in the poem it was written in the 1890s, many years after the expedition embarked, but the clarity of certain minutiae argues for first-hand knowledge.

I have checked a number of facts which relate to its veracity and have included these in an Appendix. If the account is true, then The's peaceful death in old age counteracts a large canon of proverbs in the 'Just Desserts' category. Whether these are the senile ramblings of a fantasist or the journal of a Moriartiesque serial killer I leave to the deliberation of the reader.

I should end with the suggestion that if you are of a delicate disposition, or do not want to ruin a beloved fantasy poem of your youth, you would do well not to read the following sanguine epic.

JJS October 2018

# Preface

If – and the thing is wildly possible – the charge of writing nonsense were ever brought against this author, I would be exceptionally grateful, especially if the accuser was a man of the Law. In view of the painful possibilities of anyone taking it seriously, or indeed the forty-two eradications I have carried out in a long and varied life, then I opt for the tag of Nonsense.

In essence, the well-known tale by Mr Lewis Carroll is, allowing for the poetic licence of a professional fantasist, faithful to the facts of the expedition it describes – as far as it goes. This is an indication that there had been a survivor of that ill-fated odyssey to describe it to him. The fact that I am here, stating its truthfulness, should point to the subsidiary fact that the survivor was me.

Lew and I were fellow members of the Fantod Club in London and one evening, over a range of exotic alcoholic drinks they purveyed, I related the full tale to him. He was fascinated by it and, many years later, published a version in verse to uncomplimentary reviews but great adulation by the general populace.

Lewis Carroll presented himself in public as a fascinating person, a sybaritic man of action always the centre of any gathering. I have of necessity adopted many aliases during my lifetime, as I did in this venture, but none so successfully or for so long a period as Lew, who posed as a mild-mannered cleric from Kent teaching mathematics at Oxford University without ordination or degree under the unlikely name of Charles Lutwidge Dodgson. He once told me it was an anagram of 'Godless, Ruined Gold Watch', which would have horrified its namesake. But then, the man was a wordsmith and a reality broker and would often give different rationalisations for the same fact.

He was a good friend too until we fell out over some petty disagreement. I cannot remember what it was over (Swine, Swimming or Swans) but the rift never healed.

I have always enjoyed his fantasy writing, but have the dubious pleasure of being parodied, along with my late twin Dee, in one of his books. Rather than call me 'The' he renamed me as 'Dum' in perjorative American slang.

He also filched from me and Dee the use of what he calls "portmanteau" words. These started for us at our christening by the uncle of a contemporary Oxford professor of 'Dodgson', the Reverend Spooner, who mangled our middle names during the service.

(For those of you who do not understand the nature of portmanteau words: They occur when the speaker has an equal choice in mind of two words that are consequentially enunciated as a single word which is a scrambled form of both. These can be very effective. Take, for example, the noise of a menacing dog which is something between a Snarl, a Growl or a Bark. This can be described as a Snowl, a Grark or, happily, a Snark.)

Let me shed light on one question that has long played on peoples' minds and that is: "Whatever happened to the *Cutty Snark*, did it go down with all Hands?"

As to the Ship: it suffered a change of name to the *Dying Flutchman* and was sold in Rotterdam for a useful sum of money that supported me for several years. As to the Crew: you must read the following tale. Rather than write it in straightforward prose I have written it in verse as a parody or pastiche of Lew's masterwork. Dear Lew! I am an old man now, having lived a rich and fulfilling life; and the one desire that I have left is to outlive the blighter.

The W Snark
Theophilus Willard Snark
Twasme Lodge
Crowborough Beacon

# A Start:
# The Blacking
# Of The Boots

"Just the place for a Snap," I mused, dusting the stand
Where I propped between Lightness and Dark
A sepia photograph, tinted by hand,
Of the Crew of the lost 'Cutty Snark'.

The Crew was complete, a fine herd of ten head,
Depicted 'twixt Darkness and Light
With stiff limbs and fixed grimaces, looking half-dead
Unaware that each pose was half-right.

Stern and proud stood the Bellman, a nautical swell
With raised telescope, wearing a frown
For all he could see was the brass of his Bell
Which he firmly refused to put down.

On a crate posed the Barrister, solemn though short,
Who discoursed in a stuttering treble.
He was always bewigged, even miles from a Court,
For his head was as bald as a pebble.

Standing next was the Banker, expensively clad,
Yet somehow appearing quite shabby,
A once muscular man who had gone to the bad
And was now quite amorphous and flabby.

Then the Broker, skin papyrus, body cadav'rous
As a skeleton who had been dieting:
He spoke like one too, which the rest of the Crew
Found more than a little disquieting.

# The Blacking Of The Boots

The Baker's appearance was hard to discern
For he wore a full yearsworth of garments;
Just his nose showed, which twitched, flared and wrinkled in turn;
A duplicitous sign in most varmints.

The Butcher's face looked like twin cutlets of lambs,
Like sausages over-replete
Were his fingers, all mounted on two mighty hams
Supported by flat plates of meat.

To one side sat the Beaver untying a knot.
He'd been trained in full many a task,
No-one knew how, when, where, why, by whom or for what
But none felt the impulse to ask.

The maker of Bonnets had pockets galore
Full of beads, feathers, flowers and trashery;
Like a mannequin out of a second-hand store
Specializing in weird haberdashery.

The marker of Billiards had large goggly eyes
Like the balls that were part of his trade:
He wore red and white arm bands of different size
A gilt ring, silk cravat and green shade.

And then lastly the Boots, a true ragamuffin,
With a smile that was gap-toothed and broad:
He was quite undistinguished and bland as a puffin
And, by all of the others, ignored.

That's the tally of ten, yet we're missing a notch
For one of the heads was two-faced:
One as open and true as the dial of a watch,
One as shrouded as workings encased.

The one (detailed above) appeared whiter than white
The other (unseen) deadly dark.
Who was he, the cause of the Crew's final plight?
'Twas yours truly: *Theophilus Snark.*

If you're finding my first name a bit of a mawful
Call me The, as do all of my friends
(At least my sole friend, for the rest came to awful
And unlawful bloodthirsty ends).

I, of course, used another: t'would grieve my twin brother
Deogratias Rilchiam Snark
But, sad to remember, one dark dank December
I throttled him in Regents Park.

# The Blacking Of The Boots

Begin at beginning: the aim of my plan
Was to isolate several souls
And to extract the health and the wealth of each man:
My Game had two separate goals.

As my alterly ego I launched the endeavour
Creating the Boojum and Snark.
These whimsies I floated to folks who seemed clever
But whose flaws switched their brightness to dark.

Every one had their weaknesses, many a fault
Such as snobbery, pride: But take heed!
These sins were but sprinklings of pepper and salt
Compared to the main curse – Raw Greed.

The Snark stirred cupidity, rara avidity,
With Boojum, its shadowy sibling;
And all this exotica, more than erotica,
Set every avarice dribbling.

I fed them rare tales of these creatures fictitious
Then stood back and waited, contented,
When after some days I was fed back delicious
Snark tidbits I had not invented!

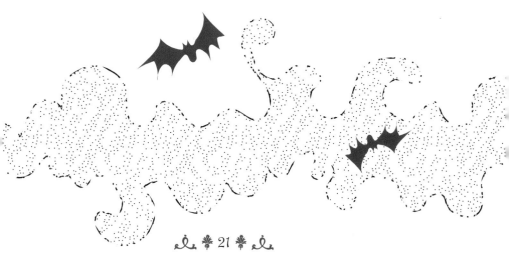

Then some hero suggested its possible capture,
This Beast worth its weight in Green Tea,
Which all of the others acclaimed with great rapture.
Who was it? Oh yes – it was me!

Next selecting the Crew (without seeming involved)
Was my hardest of tasks and quite stressful,
Like a take-apart Puzzle that had to be solved
For the whole Game to turn out successful.

I ensured that the Bellman was Crewman-in-Charge,
His fervour was hard to decry,
His status and stature impressed all at large
And his imagy-nation: oh my!

Now the ship: I'd discovered a swift sail for sale
Which would satisfy each hopeful backer,
It was perfect and trim, could face seasquall and gale
With a new name and six coats of lacquer.

The time gimbled past. Soon the crew were *en bloc*
All agog for their final *adieux*
With a *bon voyage* photograph down on the dock;
And for me *tout le monde* had their use.

What's the use of a Boots? To be perfectly blunt:
As a sacrifice to sweet success,
For once all had landed and started their hunt
He'd be first man to – "boof" – evanesce.

So great was the other Crew's pompous inflatus
That Boots was ignored by each one.
So low was his snobbish-perceived social status
That no-one would notice him gone!

If they bothered to seek him then all they would see,
Hanging out in the sun, was one boot
On the sad gnawed-off branch of a Snowberry Tree.
But they didn't. The Game was Afoot!

# Fit the First:
# The Potting Of The Billiardmarker

"Just the place for a Snap," I mused, viewing the neck
 Of the Boots as our schooner set sail.
The rest of the Crew were all milling on deck
 Or waving to friends from the rail.

I apologise, Reader, for jumping ahead
 Just now to the Boot's coming fate.
It's a Saga, so should be sequentially read
 And facts correspondingly straight.

So we're back on the ship which had bravely set forth
 As the Crew gave a rollicking cheer;
But which way it was heading – East, West, South or North
 Not one had the slightest idea!

I proposed South by North (which I took as a gift
 For S N begins the name SNark)
And, despite dogged doldrums and AntaRcticK drift,
 We should soon cross a bight in our barque.

# The Potting Of The Billiardmarker

I at least knew our target, a tropical isle
Decked with forests, volcanos and peaks.
I kenned fauna and flora, I'd stayed there a while
Marooned in my youth for ten weeks.

I sailed, when I was young, with Fleabeard the Unsung
Who was fiercer than many monsoons.
Do you need an irate and merciless pirate?
Try filching his filthy doubloons!

I was dumped on this Isle and as likely as not
Would yet be there as stranded as Crusoe
If my only true friend had not stolen a yacht
And found me when none else would do so.

That is where we were bound which took days (quite a few)
Then some weeks, then a couple of hours.
I used this prime time for observing the Crew
In all weathers – sun, squalls and showers.

To *use* men, appraise them, each strength and each wile.
Thus: at cards one was rarely defeated –
The marker of Billiards – who won in great style
And, when he was losing, he cheated!

In the 'Victims Pack' he was then shuffled to second,
(A stacked deck in which I'm the Joker),
From the Hunt I then cut him; I smilingly beckoned,
Suggesting a pause and some Poker.

First he won a few hands then he lost and he lost
Then he cheated and lost even quicker.
He could not understand it (alas to his cost)
He was slick – but then I was much slicker.

In pique he imparts a Flush Royal[1] in Hearts
To himself, with a counterfeit grin,
Purrs, "I've got you this time, so I bid my last dime
And my everything else. Are you in?"

I look at my cards which are great but not grand,
A Flush, not the best by a mile,
But I murmur, "Why not?" and I lay down my hand.
He shows his with a crocodile smile.

"Well that's life," he observes, "some you cheer, some you jeer;
I'll take all to your very last penny!"
"Just a moment," I claim, "We have ten Hearts right here
And four last hand. That's one Heart too many."

He's stunned, racked by recklessness on his own part,
He swears innocence on his foul life.
I reply, "I'll believe it if I cross your heart
And I should." And I did – with my knife.

I slumped the cadaver on a slab of lava
With his cue poised for action in hand
And three balls in a line like a pawnbroker's sign:
The heartless Billiardier's last stand.

And his heart? That I potted and salted withal
To be eaten with cucumber cues
And marrowfat peas, each depicting a ball,
Mildly mindful of my Ps and Qs.

# Fit the Second:
# The Knotting Of The Bonnetmaker

"Just the place for a Snap," I mused, as it turned cold
And noses all turned Oxford blue,
"It should stiffen our sinews and make us more bold.
What I tell you three times is – achoo!"

This phrase was the Bellman's. He'd stumble in speeches
And often repeat some points twice,
But this tag made folk say, 'He has practised his preaches,'
And wrung virtue out of a vice.

Again, gentle reader, I'm forced to say sorry
For skipping time in the last Fit.
It was just my impatience, you don't have to worry,
It won't happen again – please don't quit.

We are back on the ship where the cold froze men's eyes,
So, to cheer them, a riddle to crack:
"Why is Ice like some Cards or some Wolves or some Lies?"
No-one solved it – each come in a Pack!

The cold snap was short, the last iceberg floed by
And sank with a pitiful grark.
The Crew soon warmed up and continued to try
To practice their moves to catch Snark.

They were fencing with Forks and they argued in pairs
As to what should be done with the Soaps;
They were fumbling with Thimbles and shuffling their Shares
(The Banker's idea) with false Hopes.

The ship met all claims. The men gave it pet names
Which was seen as a meaningful mark
Of respect. The most loyal proclaimed it *Snark Royal*,
The others preferred *Nowhere Snark*.

Since our blank map was useless we steered by each star:
North by Bull and then South by Big Bear,
East by Billycock, West by bright Budgerigar.[2]
Ere you'd said "Twinkling Bats" we were there.

The Crew cheered again (They would do that a lot)
Then strung flags that they'd made for a lark.
They were blank as the Map with a red central blot:
The Bunting (they smirked) of the Snark.

The landing was hard (for the Barrister most)
But at last all were safe in a bay:
A speech that was pointless, a soul-stirring toast
And we all set out after our prey.

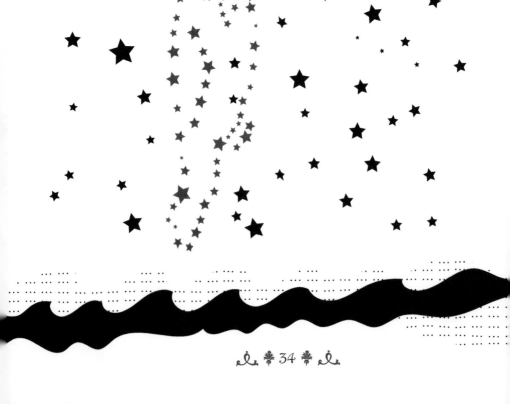

# The Knotting Of The Bonnetmaker

An hour then passed – two down, seven to go.
The maker of Bonnets seemed next.
He was still beached, perfecting his stylish death bow
So I broached him without a pretext.

I watched for a second and then drolly reckoned
That his bow would be helped by an arrow.
He sniffed, "Bows do not fit on a bowstring one bit;
Just knots, for the cord is too narrow."

"Now we're talking of knots," I posed, "how many ways
Can a four-in-hand neckpiece be tied?"[3]
"We've discussed this at Knots Club for several days,
There are just eighty five," he replied.

"The 'Man on the Clapham Bus' thinks there's but one,"
I exclaimed, "Though of course this means nix.
Still, your fellows in knottery are not spot on:
There are in fact eighty-and-six!"

He did not believe it, responded with vim,
Intertwining some feathers and fluff,
For each variation had been tied by him;
That was all and that was quite enough.

My Daedalian data I'd gained when quite youthful
Whilst lodged with a skilful knot-wrangler
In Sing Sing. They hanged him but, to be quite truthful,
I've long missed the Steershallows Strangler.

So I counselled the Bonneteer, "Let me reveal
This slip knot that I call 'the Ketch'.
It's simpler to shew you that it's really real
Than describing or making a sketch."

I selected raw silk (so much stronger than steel)
Which I wrapped round his neck not to slip
And tied knots in a manner I may not reveal.
Note: the Ketch was not named for a ship.[4]

# The Knotting Of The Bonnetmaker

For the Ketch was a slip knot which slipped by itself
And pressed on his throat ere he knew it.
He croaked, "Get it off!" I replied with a cough
I'd not yet found a way to undo it.

It grew tighter and scrunched till his windpipe was crunched
And his tongue became fully extended,
Then it turned chalky white, such an unwelcome sight
I was glad when the whole thing had ended.

I embellished his hat with three cards that opined,
'Why Knot?' and 'Why Not?' and 'Whine Not!'
And left him there fashioned for others to find.
Six more Crew still awaited their Lot.

# Fit the Third:
# The Trials
# Of The Barrister

"Just the face for a Shark," I said, tracking each snore
To the spot where the Barrister lay.
I really abhor such a man of the law
For more reasons than I care to say.

He slept in the shade of a False Alibush
Like an innocent baby or two.
His snores, like jammed doors that you pull and then push,
Drew me and one more of the Crew.

He was lucky indeed how Fate's dice had been cast
(For now at least) for his own sake;
If we'd been two Jubjubs then he would have passed
From Asleep to Awake to a Wake.

How best to arouse him? One way would be dousing
In water or giving a yell,
By prodding, thought poking might be too provoking,
So we finally opted for Bell.

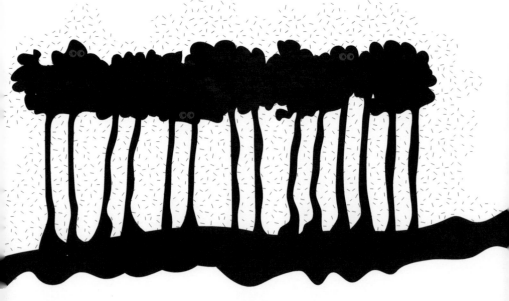

Straight upwards he sprang from the Bell's noisy clang
Coming down on a sharp Jabberthorn.
He screamed legal oaths till the glade also rang
Then found himself looked on with scorn.

Ignoring our looks he broke into a tale
Of the dreaming from which he'd awoke.
It concerned a dead pig and a Snark and a jail,
And he wrung his curled wig while he spoke.

Then before we could ask (and take him to task)
Why this nap after sailing for weeks?
Why this flagging and lagging and rank lollygagging?
From afar came ear-shrivelling shrieks.

"He's all yours, I'll check that," said the other and hurried
To where someone yelled for dear life.
The Barrister, wide awake, looked somewhat worried
As I sheathed Fork and unsheathed a Knife.

"Whilst you appeared dead to the world," I then said,
"Someone cruelly slew a few Crew;
There must be a Trial, I'll take no denial,
And the corpus on trial is you."

He tried to depart but stopped, pinked by my Knife.
"You're a vile man of parts, I submit,
And since you're on trial for your very life
You must prove lack of guilt for each bit."

The first was the Trial[5] by blest **BREAD AND CHEESE:**
That was no choke. Next, Trial by **BEAN:**
He did not expire, but started to wheeze
And turned a cruciferous green.

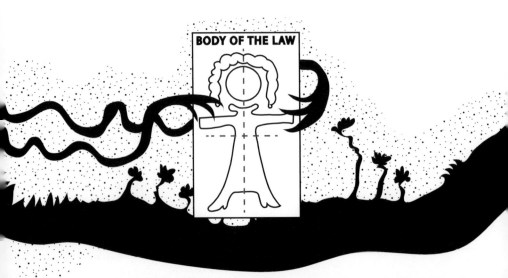

Third, Trial by BOILING OIL: searing his arm.
Then Trial by BARREL: in which
He was plunged into water, three times is the charm,
'Til he crawled out as white as a lych.

Lastly Trial by BOOJUM: constricting the bones,
Hard to tell once the process began
If the creaks and the groans and the squeaks and the moans
Were mechanical or made by man.

When at last he was clear I accorded a cheer;
He had triumphed, what more can be said?
"You're Not Guilty," I cried, but he never replied
Being incomprehensibly dead.

Thus he was, so it seems, well-intentioned at heart
This lawyer who'd idly been slaughtered
And so, as a person of many a part,
He was not hung or drawn – just Quartered.

# Fit the Fourth:
# The Whiting Of The Banker

"Just the space for a Sneak Attack, Bandersnatch-fashion,"
I observed, as the Banker dodged claws.
More Crew had arrived, drawn by his piercing passion,
And the Beast made off snapping its jaws.

These creatures are cowards, they'll fight a lone prey
But will flee if confronted by many.
And as for the Banker, well what can I say,
In for a Pound out for a Penny.

We tended this victim, whose face had turned Stygian
And who rattled a couple of bones;
We failed to revive him, he chawked like a pigeon
Whose craw had been stuffed full of stones.

There was nought we could do so we left him right there,
Made him comfortable as he could be,
Replaced his top hat having backcombed his hair
And carried on our hunting spree.

But one never left – thought the Banker, bereft
Of his senses and budgetary fee,
Had a future dim, slim but yet not right for him.
Who was it? Oh yes – it was me!

I checked with the Banker, said I had a notion
A Bandersnatch might sneakle back;
But that I could prevent this by mixing a Potion
So that no single one would attack.

It consisted of Grog (several 'hairs of the dog')
French mustard and mulberry jam,
Then mustard and cress (that's the key to success)
Til the mixture stank like rotting clam.

He never complained, so his waistcoat I stained
With globules of white, gooey Mix.
He had never smelt worse. Then I lifted his purse
Which held eighteen pounds nineteen and six.

His reactions were nil, I tried many a way
To discourse, such as Morse or Dumb Crambo.
I interlocuted, "Dry Bones do not pay;
Pound this and become Brother Tambo."[6]

This was an old tambourine tuned to B Sharp,
Which note makes a Bandersnatch run.
Then I hurriedly hid by the edge of a scarp
For safety, and viewing the fun.

Now, some things I just said might not be quite true:
That Mix? 'Snatches' favourite snack!
And they muster to B Sharp! But true as Tove stew
Was that no single one would attack.

First two and then four and then more and then more –
A Fruming of vile Bandersnatch –
Came creeping and crawling from forest and shore
Lured on by the pitch from this patch.

They followed their ears to this sad mimsy dell
Then rapidly switched to their noses,
For the sharpest of all of the senses is smell
And the Potion to them smelt like roses.

They pounced all at once with a spleen-splitting splat
And the Banker was hidden from sight,
Till all that was left was his lonely black hat
Which had turned unexpectedly white.

# Fit the Fifth:
# The Reducing
# Of The Baker

"**N**ot the place to be Stark," I just managed to gag
    Whilst my heart well and truly outgrabe,
For the Baker was prancing on top of a crag
    And he was as bare as a babe!

He had kept all his wear in this tropical air
    (Self-baking by Sun overhead)
Now, as suicides strip just before their last trip,
    He had weirdly removed every shred.

There were none as obsessed with our prey as this mark
    And his rich uncle, one of our backers,
They believed every word about Boojum and Snark
    But then they were, both of them, crackers.

Ahead of the pack he had seen something strange
    Which he pointed at, chuckling with glee.
The others peered, but it was out of their range.
    What was it? Oh yes, it was me!

"It's a Snark!" was the sound that first came to their ears
    And seemed almost too good to be true
Then followed a torrent of laughter and cheers:
    Then the ominous words "It's the Boo-"[7]

Then silence, as if he had choked in full throttle,
Or his tongue had become somehow loose:
In fact the real reason was quite epiglottal
Compressed by my lariat's noose.

I had learned to lasso long ago on the Prairie
Where I once rode with Whiskers the Kid:
I had learned to be fast, singleminded and lairy
And it was a good thing that I did.

I, quick as a flash, looped his throat with my lash
And pulled him out into thin air
Then deftly, by George, dropped him into a gorge;
They'd not find his body down there.

Now time really counted. As body count mounted
Survivor count got less and less,
And, in this condition, then mortal suspicion
Becomes mankind's favourite guess.

# Fit the Sixth:
## The Tail
## Of The Beaver

"Just the space for a Spark," I claimed, striking a light
And setting the kindling ablaze.
The Baker was lost, it was heading t'wards night
And the air was beginning to haze.

The Bellman and Broker sat East, whereupon
The Butcher and Beaver sat West.
We wondered where all of the others had gone
And what should be done for the best.

We decided to separate and try to find
And bring back the rest to the fire,
Except for the Beaver whom we'd leave behind
To stoke so it would not expire.

So we all three set off, though perhaps I should say
That, when I refer to all three,
There was one of us waited 'til two moved away.
Who was it? Oh yes – it was me!

The Beaver was *de jure* part of them all.
I, *ex parte* all of the Jury,
Found it *noxius* as sin and so should be done in
But, because it was furry, *sans* fury.

I stalked up to the Beaver with innocent Smile
But it's animal gifts did not fail
For predator-spotting. It saw through my guile
And then fled – but I snatched it's flat tail.

There's a lumberjack trick I learnt. Should Beavers fight
This vividly shortens their span:
Twist their tail six times left and then six to the right
Then hard down, and they're dead as a flan.[8]

I prepared the plump carcass with methods sublime
And left it to boil in its fat
Then constructed an alibi by buying time
And fetching the Banker's lost hat.

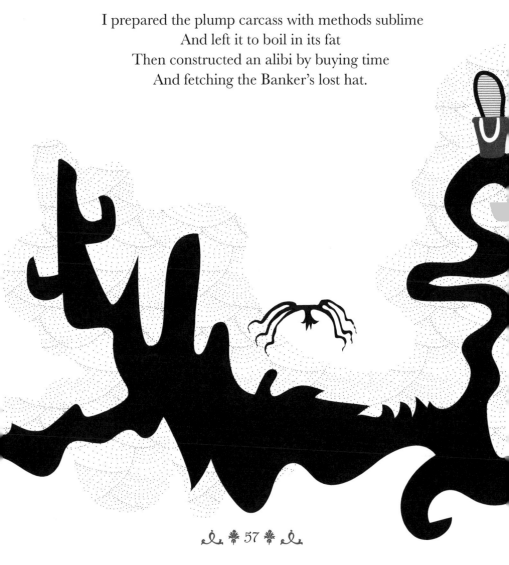

Recipe:

S k i n
the    Beaver   and
slice    it    quite    fine,
Except    for    its    tail
which        gives        flavour.
Add   sawdust,  and   more   dust,
and        garlic        and        wine
And  cloves — it's  a  taste  you  can
s    a    v    o    u    r    .
This   is   **Polluxe of Beaver**.
Add    ice   (wards   off   fever)
Submerge            in            a
S p e c i a l i z e d O i l
Then,   quick   as   a   tick,
add   a   cinnamon   stick
And      leave      half
an    hour    to
b o i l.

# Fit the Seventh
## The Breaking Of The Broker

"Just the plates for a Snack," I said, handing them round,
"When one is befuddled by shock
Then simple refreshment makes facts seem more sound –
No use going off at half cock."

The other two sat there in postures of woe,
Aghast by the things they had found.
A sad pile of objects lay there in the glow
In a circle deployed on the ground.

There were three Billiard balls and the Boot on a stick,
Three Billets retrieved from the bonnet,
The Barrister's Wig, sliced with many a nick,
And the Black Hat with whiting upon it.

"Let's recap," droned the Broker's voice, heavy as lead,
Having had a few mouthfuls of stew,
"Three murdered, three missing whom I presume dead;
And each piece in this pile is a clue."

"But what of the Beaver?" the Butcher implored.
"What indeed?" tolled the Bellman, "I thought,
The branch that impaled the Boot's boot has been gnawed,
What other sharp teeth need be sought?"

"Then what of these cards from the Bonneteer's spot?"
Grarked the Butcher to Bellman. "Not two,
But three stating: 'Why Knot?', 'Why Not?' and 'Whine Not!'
What this tells me three times is: It's you!"

"Take this billiard-ball stack," the Bellman snowled back
As his face glistered shades of red ochre.
"Arranged by design like a schlock-hock shop's sign.
That chevron points straight to a Broker."

"The Lawman was boned," the grim Broker intoned,
"Quadrisected like fine cuts of meat,
On a Butcher's shop chart limning every chopped part.
That should shew just whose guilt is complete."

But the Butcher grilled, "What of the Banker's top hat,
Once black but now covered in icing?
That proves it's the Baker, and that should be that."
Clanged the Bellman, "That would be surprising

Since we know that he's dead!" "Yes," the Broker began,
"As he fell he expressed a death rattle.
I worked in a slaughterhouse as a young man
And heard it from corrals of cattle,

And your icing is actually Bandersnatch dung."
The Bellman pealed, "Cannot you see!
These clues are all bogus!" His Bell fiercely rung
"The Assassin is one of we three!"

The silence was cracked by the Broker's distress.
He'd been helping himself to more stew,
But now dropped his plate and choked, "I must confess
I've been horribly cheating you two.

I don't believe in the Snark! I thought those who did
Were an inch short of babbling insane.
I valued your goods, but I made several quid
By shorting you now and again...

And again and again. As for this howdydo,
I can tell you the what and the how.
I can tell you the when – not the why or the who –
But I know where the Beaver is now!"

He then fished in the pail and pulled out a flat tail.
The Butcher turned red, white and blue.
He burbled, "My Beaver!" then whipped out his cleaver
And severed the Broker in two.

# Fit the Eighth
# The Butchery
# Of The Bellman

"Rest in Pieces!" A Snarl wrinkled every fat feature,
    "You boiled up my Beaver, then you
Just grinned as I ate it, you Crew-killing creature."
    The Bellman chimed, "Fudge! It's not true!

It was you singlehandedly murdered the Crew,
    And your sights are on me. I'm the next!"
"Not I," said the Butcher, "the Broker, it's true,
    But I was, as you know, sorely vexed.

He boiled my bijou Beaver into ragout."
    Quizzed the Bellman, "You're sure it was he?
For I spied you, when nearing, right here in this clearing
    Before both the Broker and me.

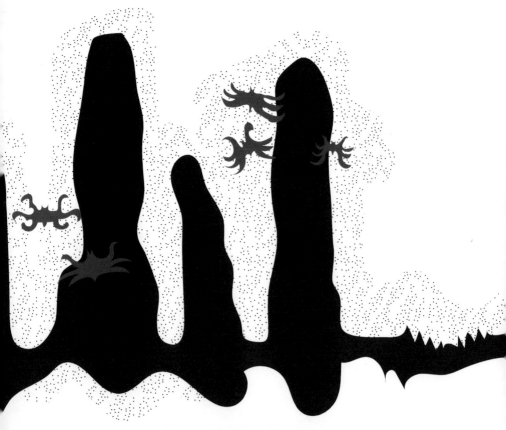

# The Butchery Of The Bellman

I assumed you were cook, you're a Butcher at least
And used to the handling of meat
So it's logical that you'd prepare such a feast
To provide us three something to eat."

But the Butcher said, "Three, eh? When out on the cliff,
Though the evening was turning raw umber,
I glimpsed Broker and Beaver, add me and then if
That makes Three it's a meaningful number."

His mind-mincer turned slowly, "Now if there's just two
And we have lost two of those Three
Then the culprit must either be me or be you,
And it weren't mathematically me."

He brandished his cleaver. I cannot pretend
That I meant such an end to this lark.
So, Good reader Goodbye from your very Good friend
And Bellman, Theophilus Snark!

"It weren't me! It weren't me!" and I turned a grey hue
"It weren't me! I mean it was not I!
There, I've said it three times..." Grinned the Butcher, "Untrue!
That was four, so we know it's a lie!"[9]

Then a voice from behind ordered, "Ten pounds of fat
If thou please: I'll make do with your head!"
The Butcher twirled round with the speed of a Bat.
I had one chance or else I was dead.

# The Butchery Of The Bellman

My Bell had a 'chess switch' that most don't possess
From Bishop to Knight fianchetto.
Off came clapper and casing and yoke with one press
Leaving only a deathly stiletto.

He'd presented his back so I stabbed for the heart
Then for liver and lights and sweetbread.
He groaned, dropped his chopper (not wise on his part)
Which was seized and then, 'Off with his head!'

In the gathering darkness I slumped on the carcass
Which was handy, to sit for a bit:
The day'd been supreme like a lilting Life dream
And the End was a near-perfect Fit.

# An End:
# The Bolting
# Of The Butcher

"Just the Place for thee, Snark," said the voice from the dark
And it chuckled and laughed in low hoots.
I'd known in the end I could count on my friend –
Aaron Boojum, alias the Boots.

He posed, framed by firelight, "I've not yet fed,
Is there nothing but Polluxe to eat?"
Then he juggled the head of the Butcher and said,
"Don't his lugs look like two steaks of meat?

'Fiends, Foemen and Counterfeits, lend us thine ears,'"
(We were fond of a good misquotation)
"They would go down quite well with some Grog or some beers
After roasting on thy conflagration."

Good reader acquit my misdealing a bit,
You've been wilfully kept in the dark.
For when you've read "me" it could be he OR me,
The brace set of Boojum and Snark.

You may have been asking, "How can just one soul
Accomplish such carnage scot-free?"
It was really two people fulfilling the role
For The Snark had A. Boojum, you see.

We equally started, the Game was Afoot,
We equally ended Ahead.
There were none to dispute this. There might have been, but
They were all of them equally dead.

We returned to the ship having bolted the meat,
Leaving all the cadavers alone:
Even strange creepy creatures need something to eat
And each corse would be stripped to the bone.

That's an End, my dear reader. Some day if I can
I will tell you about our next spree.
Who first said the Ripper was only one man?
Oh yes, I recall — it was me!

*Ludus Completus*[10]

# Appendix

**1]**

*Poker has long been a gambling staple in the USA, less so in the UK. For the non-gamblers amongst you a Royal Flush is a holding of AKQJ & Ten in the same suit. It is the highest hand one can hold, and the chances against it being dealt are just under 650,000 to 1. For a cardsharp to deal this unlikely hand to himself and a Flush of five random cards in the same suit in the same hand to his opponent is over Seventeen and a Half Billion to One against.*

*To create such a distribution is rank amateurism, and can only have been motivated by frustration or desperation.*

**2]**

*The Bull and Bear are known signs in the Western Zodiac (and, probably irrelevantly, signs of confidence and its opposite in the Stock Market.)*

*The other two are unknown in any Zodiac: so it is probable that The was attempting to hide the exact location of the island.*

*There exists a Snark Island, a quarter of a square mile in area, near to a Boojum Rock, in the Bay of Bengal: this has been visited expectantly a number of times and, alas, is not the island hoped for. It is presumably a piece of cartographical whimsy named after the creature in Carroll's book, in the same way that the weirdly-shaped Boojum Tree was christened by a capricious British ecologist.*

*Whilst in this area it should be noted that two of the Andaman Isles have softly and suddenly vanished away in the last hundred years or so. Despite its probable location on the other side of the world could The's island have suffered this fate? It would explain the frustrating inability to rediscover it and the biological treasures it holds.*

3]

In 1830 a book titled 'L'Art de la Toilette' was published describing 72 ways of tying a Cravat.

In the 1850s, the Four-in-Hand (today's basic tie) was introduced as sporting attire in a gentleman's Club of that name and gained huge popularity. Well up into the 20th Century there was only considered to be one way to tie it sartorially.

In 1867, Lord Kelvin gave a lecture to the Royal Society of Edinburgh on Knots and Vortices. This gave rise to Knot Theory and the formation of a small number of clubs attended by Mathematicians, Physicists and Sailors, and apparently Bonnetmakers.

In 1999, 100 years after The's death, Fink and Mao published the excitingly titled 'The 85 Ways to Tie a Tie', using Markovian Chain Theory and computers to verify the Knot Clubs' findings.

4]

If the Ketch was not named after a type of ship then it was presumably named after Jack Ketch, the notorious public executioner under Charles II. He hamfistedly executed a number of notables, including Lord Russell after which he published a pamphlet titled Apologie in which he justified his actions. It is worth noting that the Ketch Knot does not appear in Fink and Mao's book, which means that either it has been tactfully supressed or computers are still no match for the diabolical cunning of the infamous Steershallows Strangler.

5]

The first four trials by ordeal are genuine. Early Franconian Law prescribed the eating of a dried piece of bread and cheese that had been blessed by a priest. If the accused choked he was guilty. The Efik people of Nigeria would administer the poisonous Calabar bean Physostigma Venenosum. If the accused died he was guilty. Some villages in India placed a small coin in a bowl of boiling oil. If the accused refused to retrieve it he was guilty. In the late Middle Ages under Frankish Law the defendant was submerged three times in a barrel. If the accused floated he was guilty.

The final trial was obviously of a personal nature, and anyone more knowledgeable and less squeamish than I might learn more details by examining the equipment in The's Chest.

6]
Minstrel shows were uniformly popular in the USA from the 1850s and later in the UK. The performers would sit in a semicircle of which the end men were Brother Bones and Brother Tambo who played the bone castanets and tambourine respectively. They wore traditional blackface and conversed in gaffes and wisecracks with the Master of Ceremonies who wore traditional whiteface and was called Mister Interlocutor.

7]
This verse is almost identical to a verse from The Hunting of the Snark, save for one word which could throw light upon what the Baker was trying to say.

8]
The Beaver, from the description of its tail, is of the North American species and not the Eurasian. The method given for its disposal is highly unlikely.

It is patently impossible to run an exteriment on a species that has lost 80% − 90% of its population due to hunting; but an etymologist might consider why the author uses the word "vivid" applied to this activity.

9]
The Bellman's rule-of-three has probably been discussed more than any other part of the Carrollian poem, with multiple interpretations. The has explained it earlier in a mundane manner, but this twist on it poses an

*interesting thought. We know that The was obsessed with knotting, and in 3-dimensional space an object may be fastened with a variety of true knots. However in 4-dimensional space it is impossible to tie any knot, and so a 4-D knot would always be false!*

*X]*
*There are One Fifty stanzas in this epic verse.*
*Roman numerals scribe this C L,*
*The reverse of L C. Could this be a last curse*
*Projected at Lewis Carrell?*

*Oh gee! Carroll. (Apologee, J.J.S)*

# Why?

## (Definitive Solution)

butCher
bAker
barrIster
baNker
beAver
bonnetMaker
billiardmarker
belLman
brokEr
Boots

*The Snark was a BELLMANIAC!*

**ZZZ...** Wake up! If, as is likely, you prefer the Lewis Carroll version and have long admired and envied the intrepid band of Snark-hunters then *This Is The Game For You!*

# SNARK!

consists of over 100 casino-quality playing cards with which you can:

~ *Construct a Ship*
~ *Become a Bellman*
~ *Hire men from the Crew Deck*
~ *Hunt the Snark in the Animal Pack*
~ *And even, when you have beaten your opponent(s),* **BEWARE...**
*You may have to take on the Snark itself!*

A Game for 2, 3 or 4 Players
(but I tell you, three players is best!)

Printed in Great Britain
by Amazon

41341174R00048